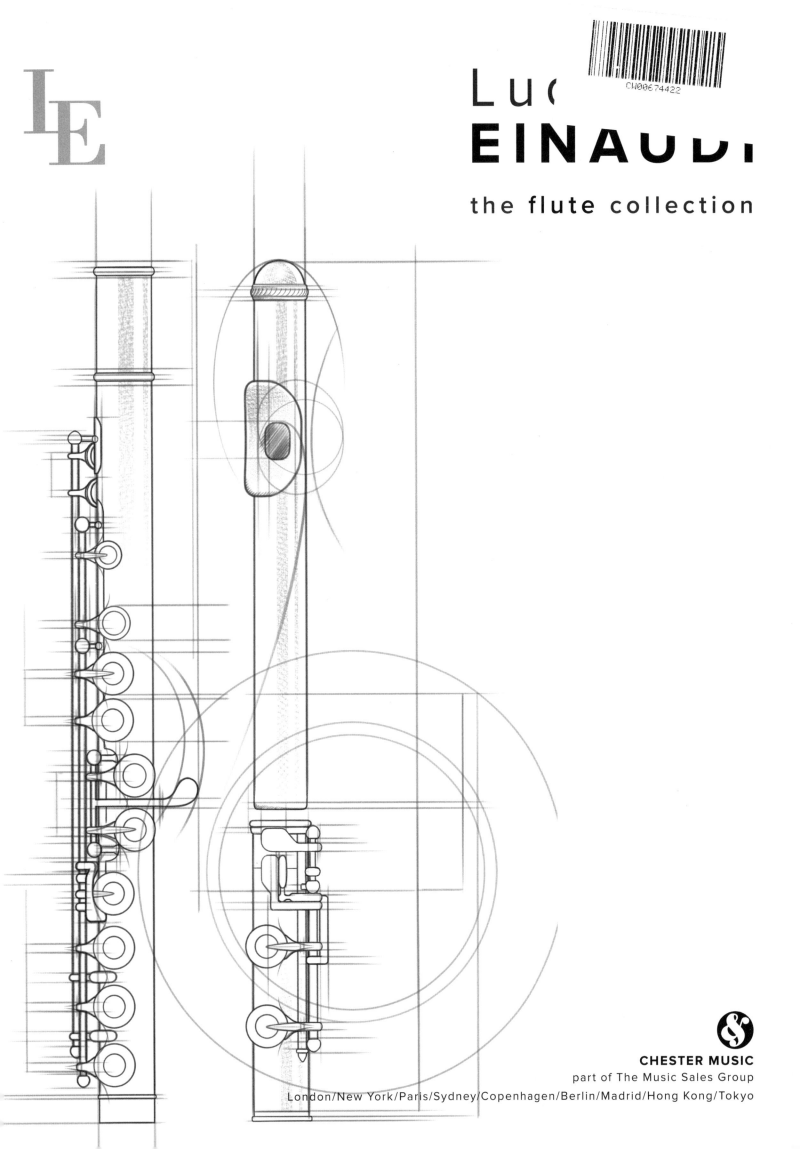

Ludovico EINAUDI

the flute collection

CHESTER MUSIC
part of The Music Sales Group
London/New York/Paris/Sydney/Copenhagen/Berlin/Madrid/Hong Kong/Tokyo

Published by

Chester Music
part of The Music Sales Group
14-15 Berners Street, London W1T 3LJ, UK.

Exclusive Distributors:
Music Sales Limited
Distribution Centre, Newmarket Road,
Bury St Edmunds, Suffolk IP33 3YB, UK.

Music Sales Corporation
180 Madison Avenue, 24th Floor,
New York NY 10016, USA.

Music Sales Pty Limited
Level 4, Lisgar House,
30-32 Carrington Street,
Sydney, NSW 2000 Australia.

Order No. CH85008
ISBN 978-1-78558-323-0
This book © Copyright 2017 Chester Music Limited.
All Rights Reserved.

Project managed by Sam Lung.
Compiled and edited by Sam Lung, Louise Unsworth and James Welland.
Arrangements by Ludovico Einaudi, Alistair Watson and Sam Lung.
Music engraved by Sarah Lofthouse, SEL Music Art Ltd.
Audio mixed and mastered by Jonas Persson.
Flute recorded by Tom Hancox.
Piano recorded by Ben Dawson.
Design by Ruth Keating.
Cover illustration by Sergio Sandoval.
With special thanks to the English Session Orchestra contracted by Jojo Arvanitis.

Printed in the EU.

www.musicsales.com

Your Guarantee of Quality

As publishers, we strive to produce every book to the
highest commercial standards. This book has been
carefully designed to minimise awkward page turns
and to make playing from it a real pleasure.
Particular care has been given to specifying acid-free,
neutral-sized paper made from pulps which have not
been elemental chlorine bleached. This pulp is from
farmed sustainable forests and was produced with
special regard for the environment.
Throughout, the printing and binding have been
planned to ensure a sturdy, attractive publication
which should give years of enjoyment. If your copy
fails to meet our high standards, please inform us and
we will gladly replace it.

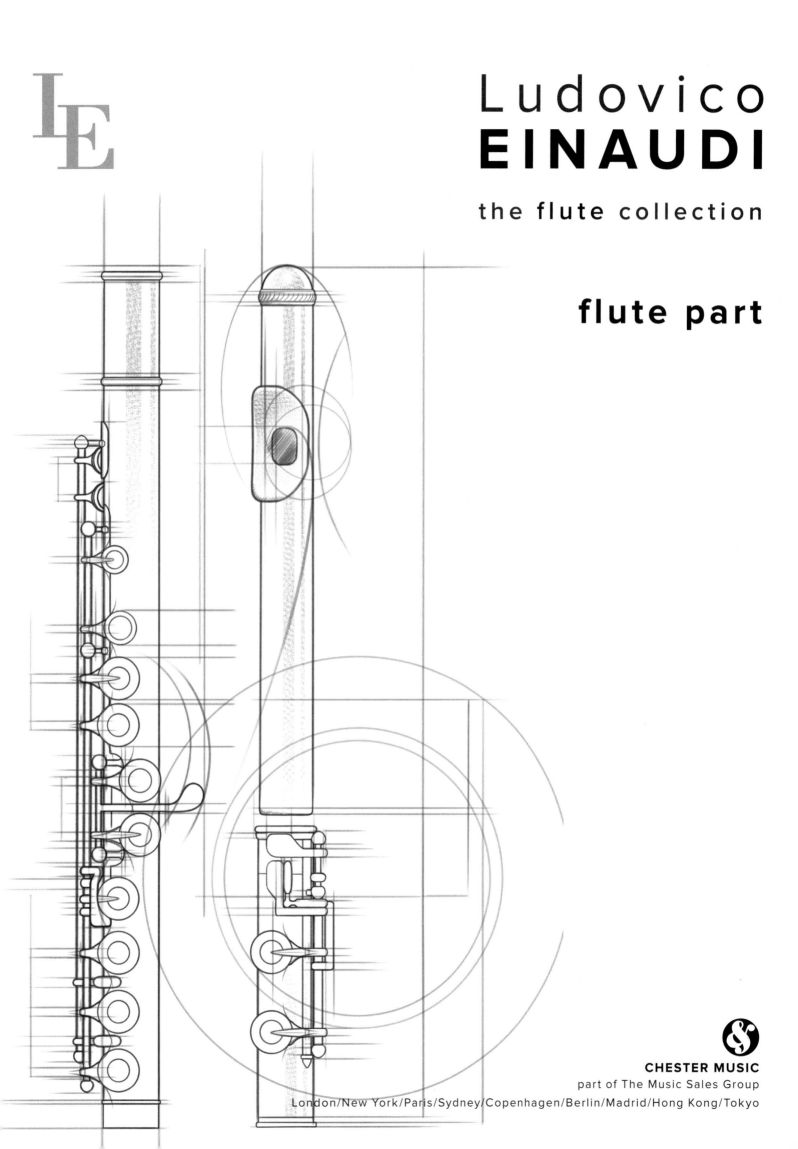

Ludovico EINAUDI

the flute collection

flute part

CHESTER MUSIC
part of The Music Sales Group
London/New York/Paris/Sydney/Copenhagen/Berlin/Madrid/Hong Kong/Tokyo

Published by

Chester Music
part of The Music Sales Group
14-15 Berners Street, London W1T 3LJ, UK.

Exclusive Distributors:
Music Sales Limited
Distribution Centre, Newmarket Road,
Bury St Edmunds, Suffolk IP33 3YB, UK.

Music Sales Corporation
180 Madison Avenue, 24th Floor,
New York NY 10016, USA.

Music Sales Pty Limited
Level 4, Lisgar House,
30-32 Carrington Street,
Sydney, NSW 2000 Australia.

Order No. CH85008-01
ISBN 978-1-78558-323-0
This book © Copyright 2017 Chester Music Limited.
All Rights Reserved.

Project managed by Sam Lung.
Compiled and edited by Sam Lung, Louise Unsworth and James Welland.
Arrangements by Ludovico Einaudi, Alistair Watson and Sam Lung.
Music engraved by Sarah Lofthouse, SEL Music Art Ltd.
Audio mixed and mastered by Jonas Persson.
Flute recorded by Tom Hancox.
Piano recorded by Ben Dawson.
Design by Ruth Keating.
Cover illustration by Sergio Sandoval.
With special thanks to the English Session Orchestra contracted by Jojo Arvanitis.

Printed in the EU.

www.musicsales.com

Your Guarantee of Quality

As publishers, we strive to produce every book to the
highest commercial standards. This book has been
carefully designed to minimise awkward page turns
and to make playing from it a real pleasure.
Particular care has been given to specifying acid-free,
neutral-sized paper made from pulps which have not
been elemental chlorine bleached. This pulp is from
farmed sustainable forests and was produced with
special regard for the environment.
Throughout, the printing and binding have been
planned to ensure a sturdy, attractive publication
which should give years of enjoyment. If your copy
fails to meet our high standards, please inform us and
we will gladly replace it.

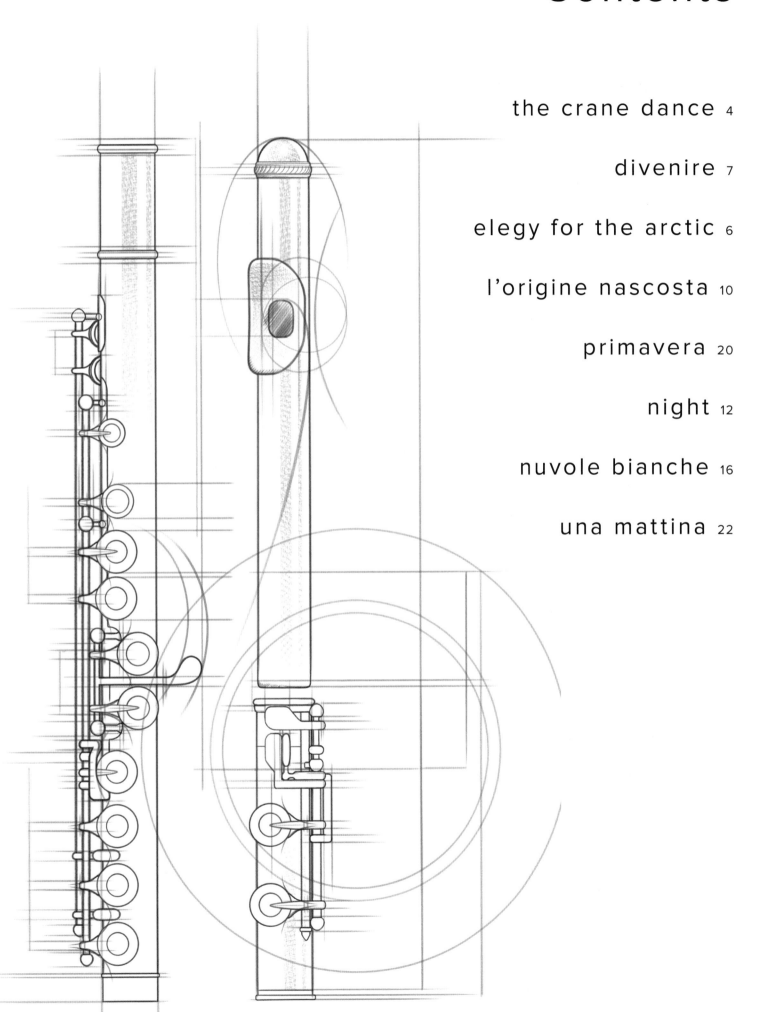

Contents

the crane dance

LUDOVICO **EINAUDI**

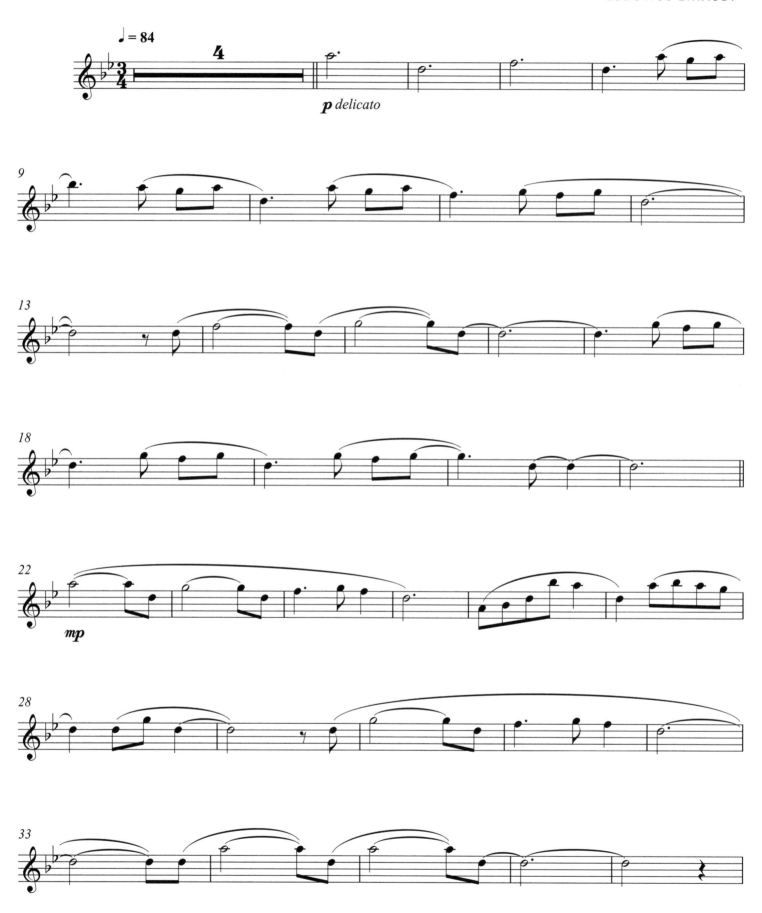

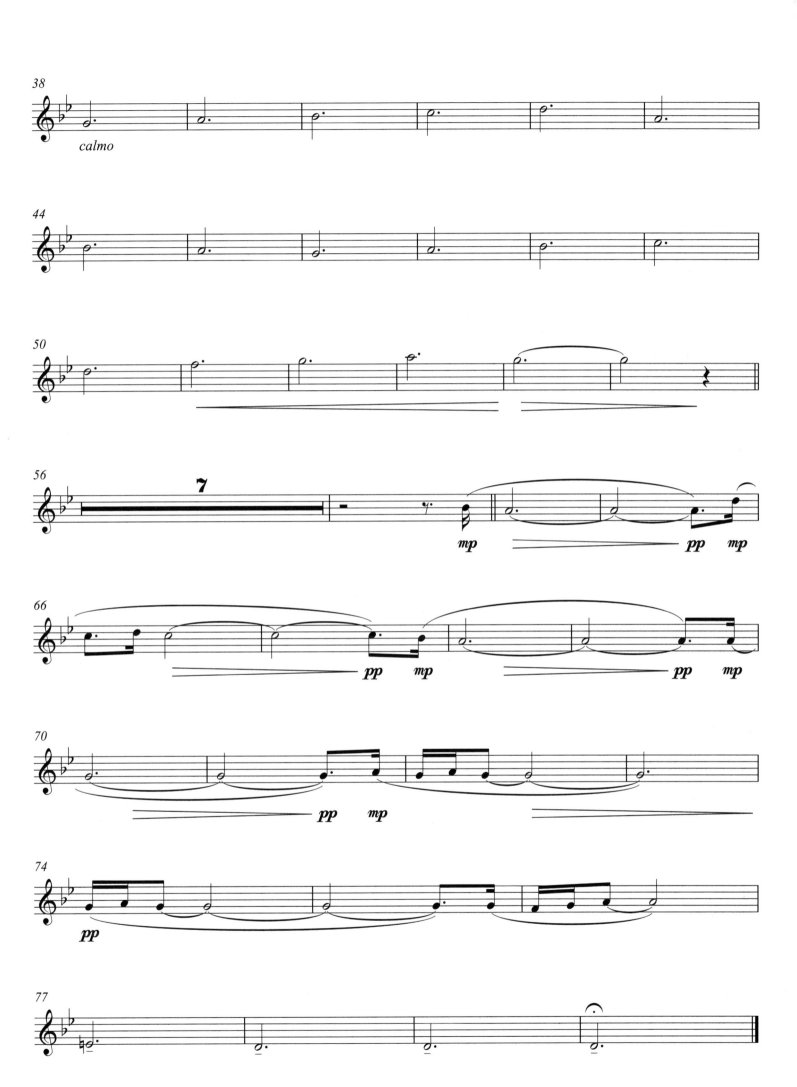

flute solo

elegy for the arctic

LUDOVICO **EINAUDI**

flute solo

divenire

LUDOVICO **EINAUDI**

7

8

l'origine nascosta

LUDOVICO **EINAUDI**

night

LUDOVICO **EINAUDI**

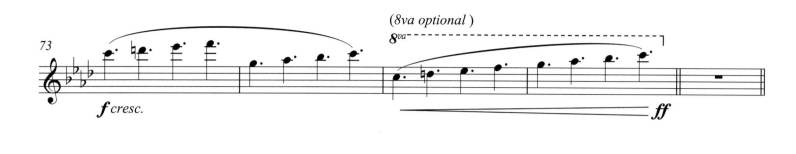

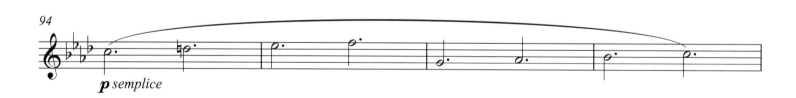

nuvole bianche

LUDOVICO **EINAUDI**

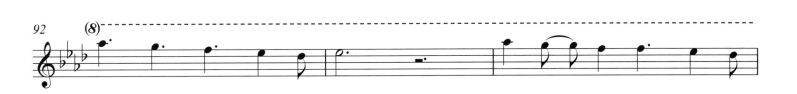

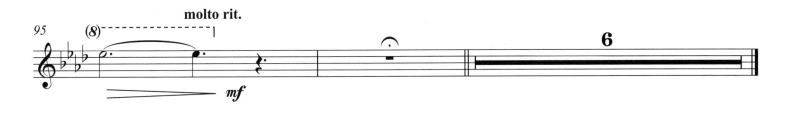

primavera

LUDOVICO **EINAUDI**

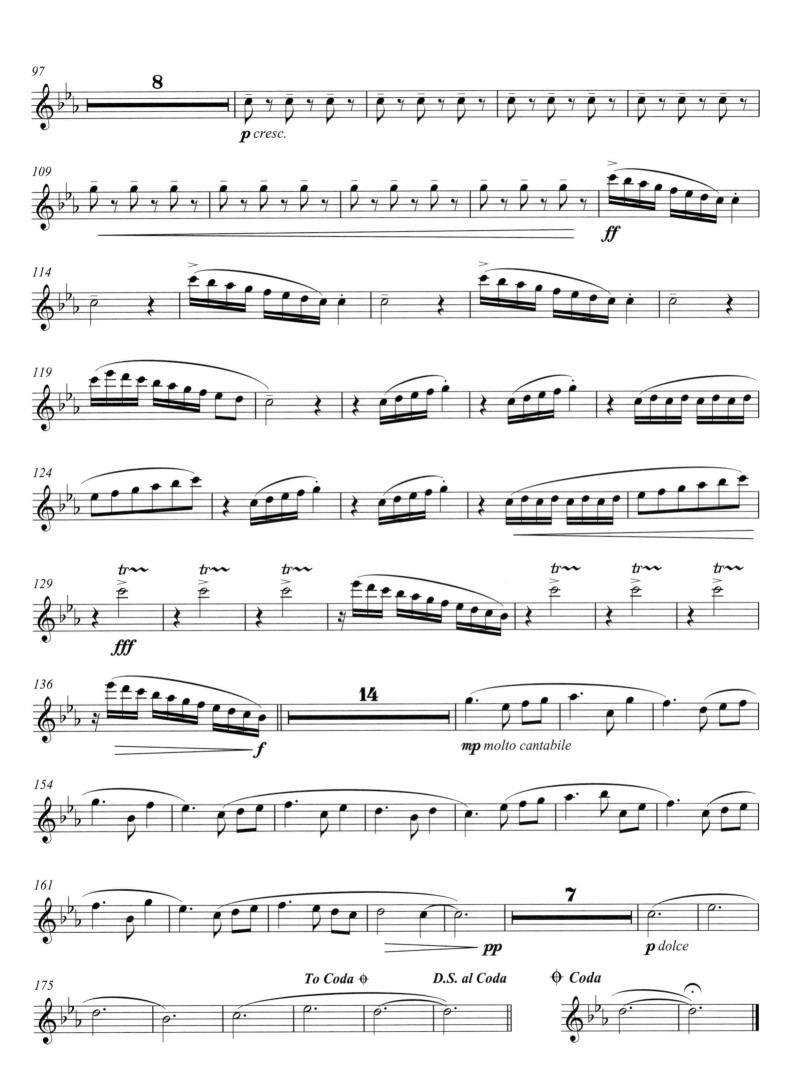

una mattina

LUDOVICO **EINAUDI**

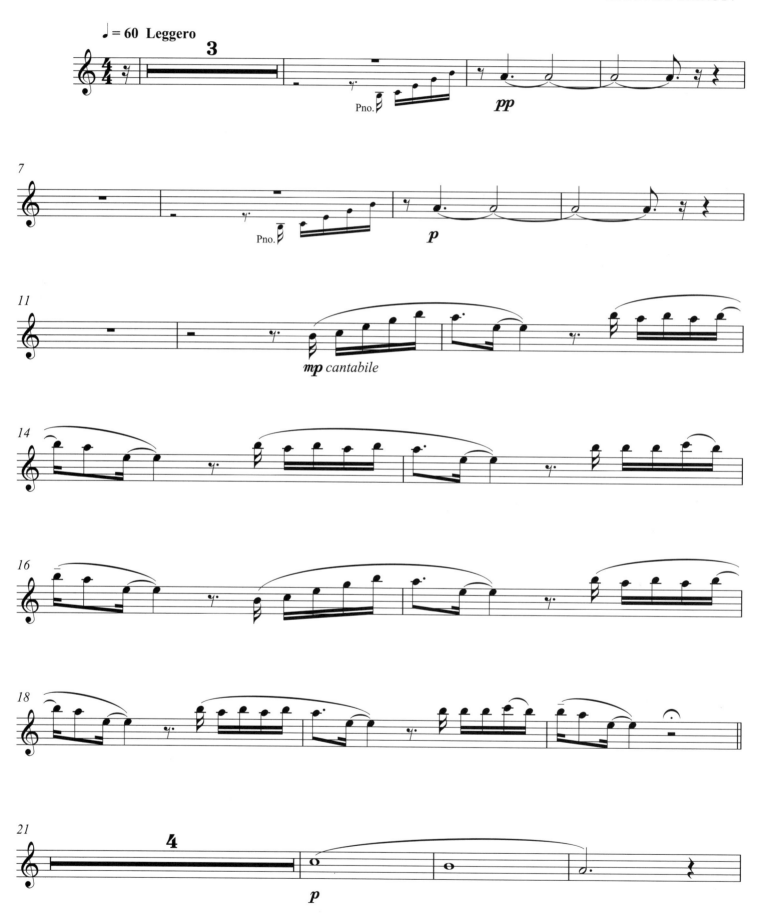

poco cresc.

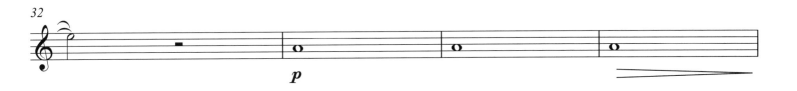

p

cantabile

2

ppp

rit.

1 2 3 4 5 6 7 8 9

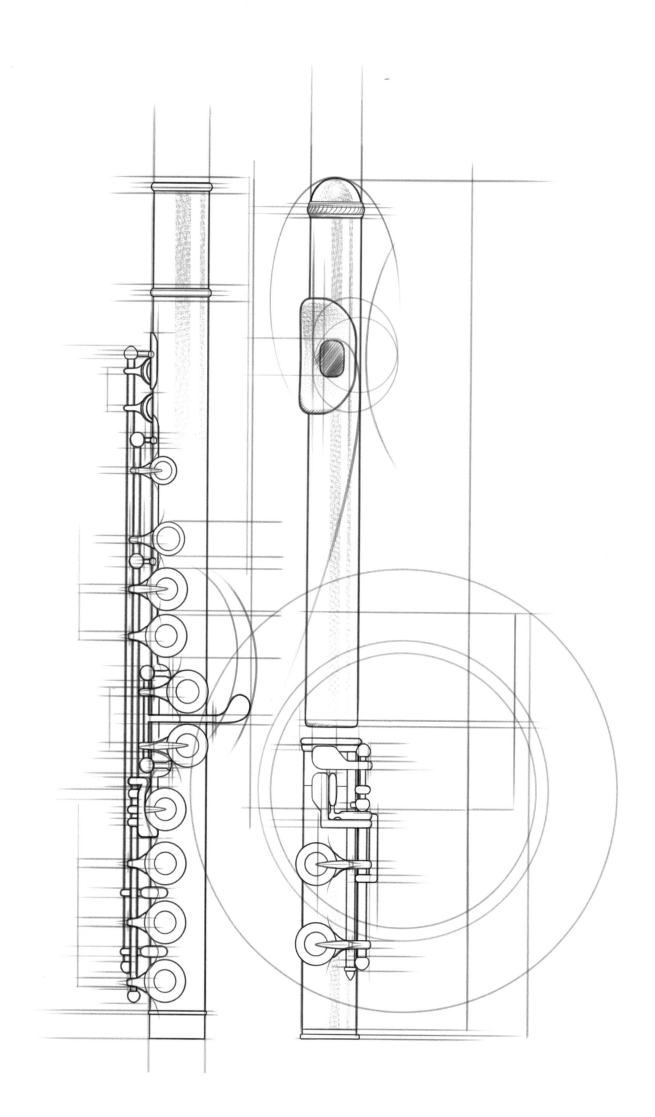

Contents

the crane dance

LUDOVICO **EINAUDI**

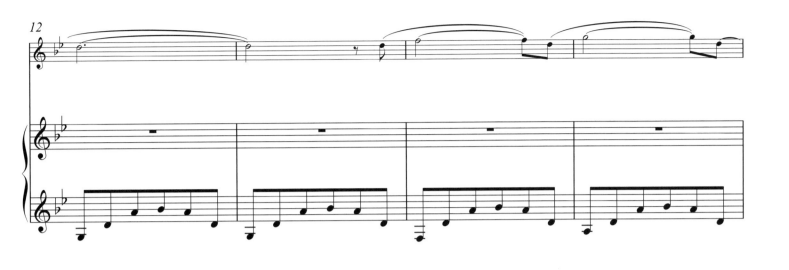

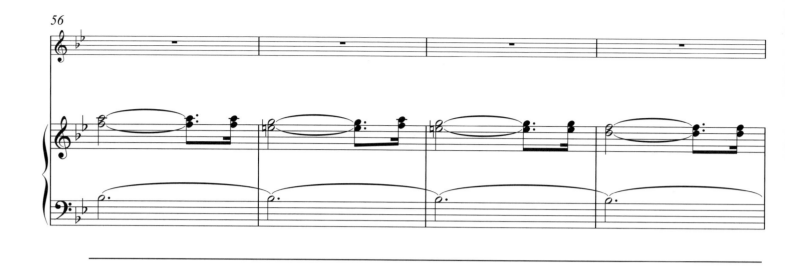

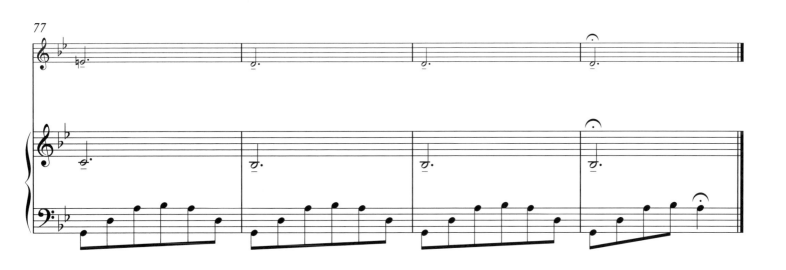

elegy for the arctic

LUDOVICO **EINAUDI**

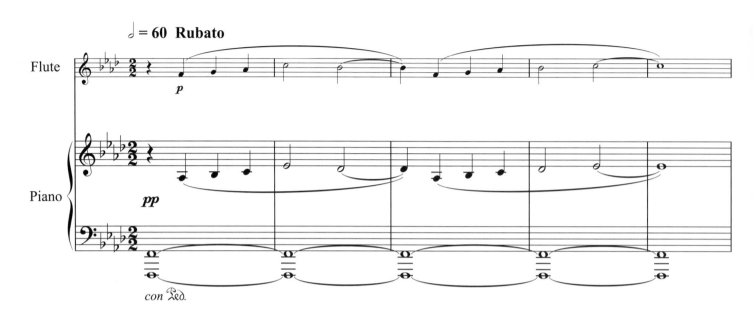

divenire

LUDOVICO **EINAUDI**

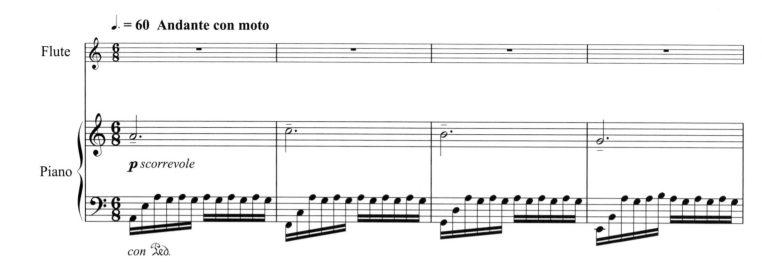

l'origine nascosta

LUDOVICO **EINAUDI**

night

LUDOVICO **EINAUDI**

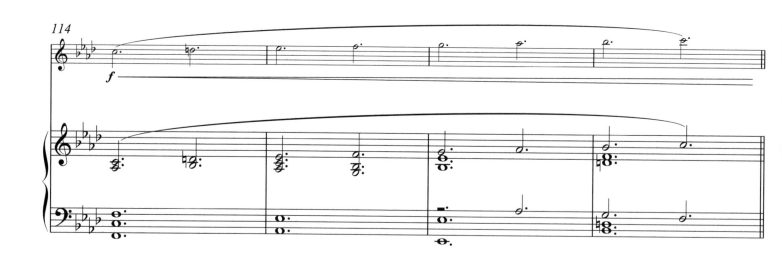

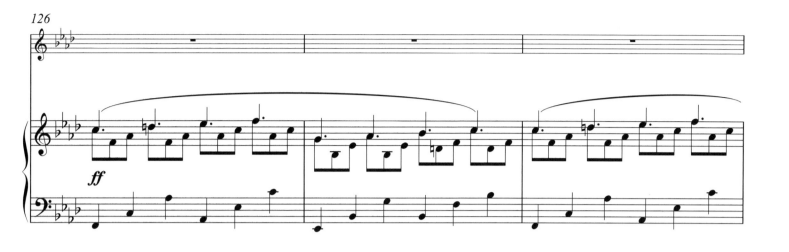

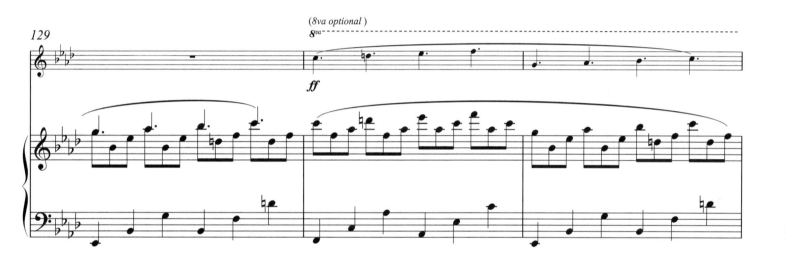

nuvole bianche

LUDOVICO **EINAUDI**

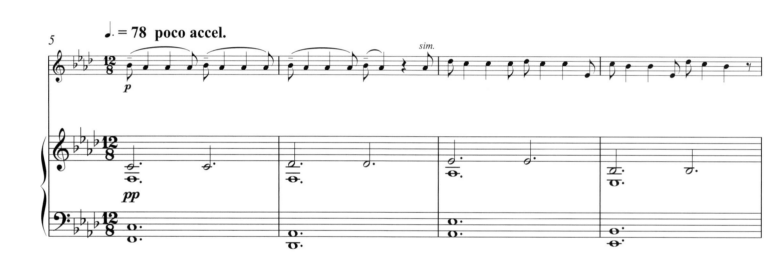

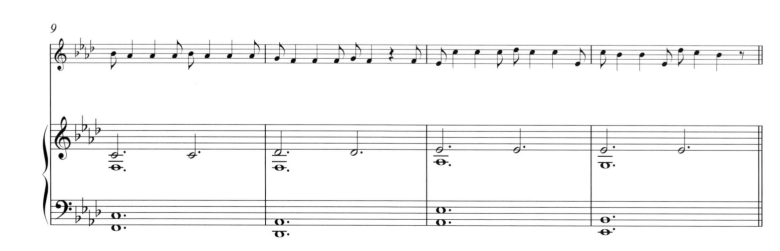

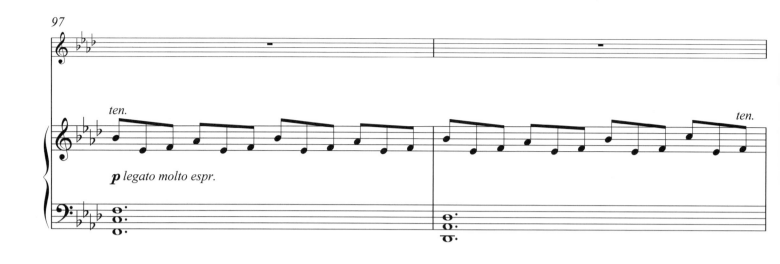

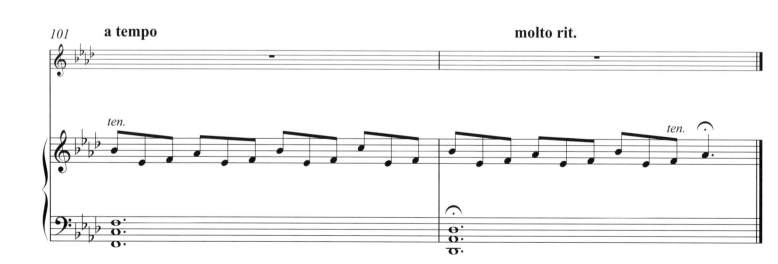

primavera

LUDOVICO **EINAUDI**

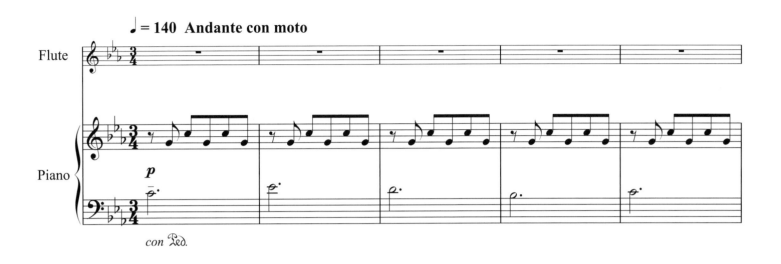

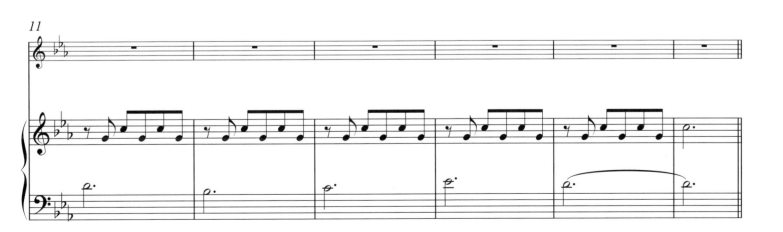

una mattina

LUDOVICO **EINAUDI**

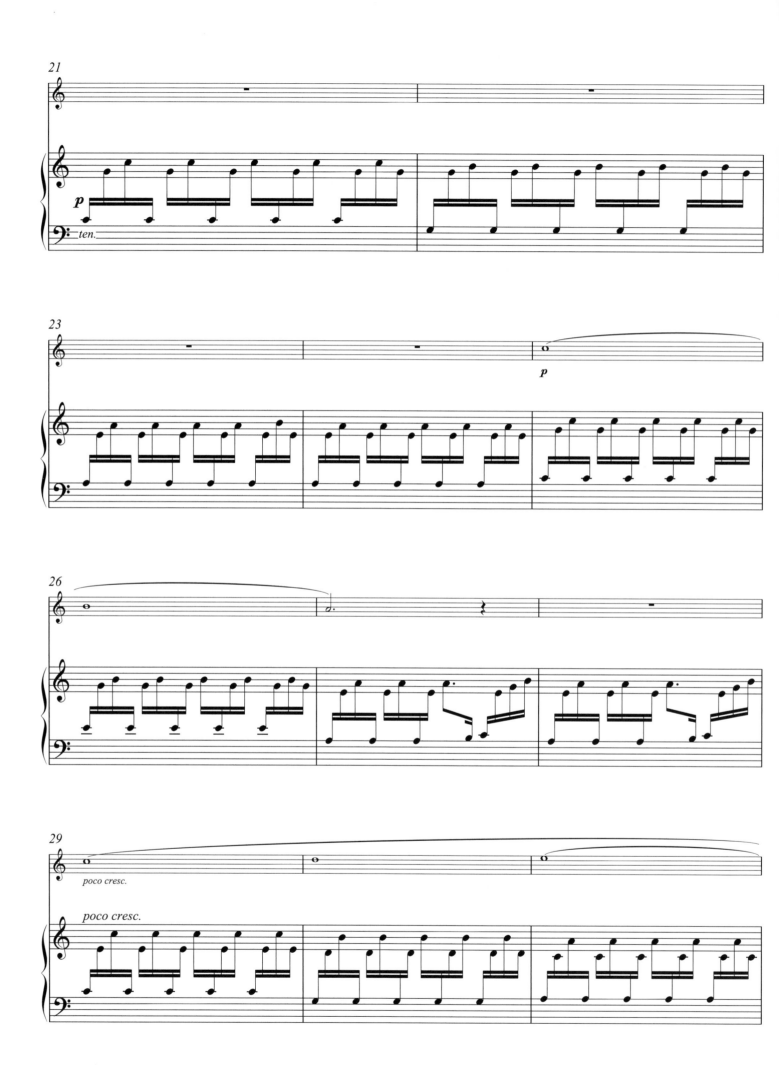